To Ju

Michigan
Memories

You brother

Dave

Michigan Memories

Hunting and Fishing Tales

By
Dave Van Til

E-BookTime, LLC
Montgomery, Alabama

Michigan Memories
Hunting and Fishing Tales

ISBN: 978-1-60862-414-0

First Edition
Published July 2012
E-BookTime, LLC
6598 Pumpkin Road
Montgomery, AL 36108
www.e-booktime.com

Contents

Contents

Mine or Yours

Dewey pulled another gill through the ice. He'd gotten to the lake at daylight and already had a dozen gills flopping on the ice.

While baiting his hook he heard a door slam, then another. "Shoot, I forgot to lock my doors," he thought. "I wonder who is monkeying with my truck."

He packed his gear and hurried to his truck and saw someone standing next to it. "What now?" he thought. "I've got permission to fish here, I wonder who this is?"

"Dewey Long?" he asked.

"Yes."

"You are trespassing on my property, and I called the police. They are on their way," the man said.

"I've got permission," Dewey said.

"Not anymore," the man replied. "You had permission from my dad, and he's dead. I own this property now."

"How'd you know my name?"

"I got it from your registration in your glove book and I'm putting an end to this trespassing now."

Dewey's mind raced as he thought what to do, then a wry smile came over his face. "Mister, I may get a ticket for trespassing, but I'm pressing charges against you for breaking and entering." Then, glancing at his wife's purse lying on the seat he said, "And stealing! I'm going to look in her purse for that 100 dollar bill, and it had better be there, or I am pressing charges against you!"

The man was stunned! "Dewey, I didn't take any money from that purse. I didn't even look in there."

Dewey replied, "I'm not trespassing either. I had permission from your dad so I guess we're at a draw. It's your call." Dewey loaded his gear into his truck then drove out. As he was driving down the road, he met a county cruiser.

"Why? Why do people have to be that way?" Dewey thought. "I never did any harm to that property, yet because the property changed 'ownership' I can't use it anymore."

Cold Snow Coon

My wife, my oldest son Todd and I were sitting around one late November evening, bored. Our youngest son Dave was visiting a friend, and there was nothing on TV.

I said, "Hey, does anyone want to go coon hunting?" They both looked at me like I was nuts. I had been gone for many, many nights through October and November.

They said, "Why? Why? Why do you have to go hunting?"

"Because I want to share a good hunt with you."

The night was cold, clear, and snowy. It was not good for coon hunting, but we needed the exercise.

The dogs were ready, for they hadn't been out in a week. After loading the dogs, we headed for a swamp on the east end of Crane Road. We were hunting with Gleem, a nine year old Bluetick, and her two-year old pup, Dusty.

Dusty was the runt of Gleem's litter. She had been born with just one eye. The other had just a socket hole, but no eyeball. She was an excellent track and tree dog. Gleem was a hardheaded old dog, but she could take a cold track, work it up, then tree the coon. She ran trash, (possum and deer), but was a good coon dog when the coon were moving.

We unleashed the dogs, then waited for them to strike. The night was very cold as we waited for their voices. The cold snap that we had the previous week had frozen all the small ponds. The moon was full as it peeked up over the horizon. "The Big Yellow is coming up," my hunting partner, Sonny, would say.

When the "Big Yellow" was coming up it generally wasn't good coon hunting, because the deer move at night during the full moon. The coon also move, but seem cautious and hard to tree.

The dogs drifted through the woods, but didn't strike. We walked to Big Bear Swamp, where there were plenty of den trees.

Gleem struck first with one long drawn out bawl, then another. The track definitely wasn't hot, but then, neither was the night. Dusty finally opened. The track was warming up a bit.

They moved away from the den area, crossing a patch of woods. The scent was getting warmer. They were moving a warm track on a cold night.

They were both pushing the coon now. I hoped the coon wouldn't double back to the den tree, as they often do on cold nights. He didn't have a chance, as they were pushing him hard now, he would have to climb. I heard Gleem locate the tree first. Then both dogs were chopping hard, saying, "Over here, over her. We found him. Come on, come on."

We headed for their barking, wondering where they had treed for the area they were treeing didn't have any big trees. The coon may have just tapped a tree and gone on.

We walked to the edge of a small, frozen shallow pond where the dogs had treed. The trees in it were very small, and I thought I saw a hump up one of them. There he was. He hadn't had time to get back home. The dogs had pushed him up that short scrub on a moonlit night.

We had treed coon on a cold moonlit night! There is one thing for sure; you can't catch fish if your line is not in the water. And you can't tree coon if you're lying on a couch watching TV.

Gramps is Always Right?

I wasn't sure what I heard when I was introduced to my wife's grandpa. I had just said hello to her grandparents. Her grandmother said hello but all I heard from him was a muffled grunt.

We were just married and were traveling north on our honeymoon. Not having much money we stayed at some motels and some relatives. We arrived at her grandparents' home late one evening. We sat around for awhile then went upstairs to an ice cold bedroom.

We got up the next morning, had breakfast, sat, and talked a little; a very little. I looked outside and saw a nice fresh snowfall had fallen during the night. I asked gramps if there were any rabbits around.

"Naw," he said.

"Would you mind if I borrowed a gun to check it out for myself?"

"Naw," he said. Then he went and got me a single shot 12 gauge, and 2 shells.

Wow, I thought, what a generous man. He's going to let me use his gun and 2 whole shells.

"You won't need more shells than this, 'cause there ain't no rabbits," he said.

Heading out through the snow, the sun was shining and the world was bright, and beautiful. I walked toward a small cedar swamp, north of the house.

My eyes had to adjust to the darkness as I made my way into the dense cedar swamp. I remembered being in a cedar swamp once before, when I was 16 years old, and was deer hunting in an unfamiliar area. Not having a compass, I had wandered into a cedar swamp. I wasn't afraid of getting lost for there was plenty of snow to backtrack. There wasn't much snow in the depths of the swamp and I lost my way by not paying attention. The night was coming quickly and the dense swamp made it darker quicker. I became desperate. I started walking faster, and faster, trying to find my way out. I was deer hunting, but I wasn't deer hunting. I was hunting a way out. Then, I jumped a big buck. I didn't even fire a shot at him for I was scared and lost. I finally made it to the road, but I still had 3 miles to walk to my parking spot.

This time it was different. I had plenty of light, and I was enjoying myself as I wandered around the swamp, looking here and there. I found where a porcupine had made a big pile of droppings under its den tree.

I caught a movement out of the corner of my eye. Something white had moved. I wondered if it was a bird or an ermine. Quietly, I moved to the spot where I'd seen the movement. A big white rabbit took off from a clump. I had time for one shot. I connected. Walking over, I picked up my first snowshoe hare.

Proud of my catch, I walked back to the farmhouse. Grandpa was leaning against the back door as I approached, with my rabbit in hand.

"You must have gotten the last rabbit in the county," he said. "I didn't know there were any left."

I cleaned the rabbit, went in, and sat down. Gramps warmed up right after that. We rode many miles in his old pick-up as he showed us all his special places, the elk crossings and the bear trees, with claw marks on them.

Later that evening, we loaded our suitcases, then said our goodbyes. I actually heard him say good-bye.

Bobcat

The morning was beginning to break as we headed down a northern Michigan two-track. Bob, who was driving, turned to me and asked, "Do you think we'll find a track?" The track we were looking for was the elusive bobcat.

The previous three hours we had spent driving from southern Michigan to the upper counties, where bobcat hunting had opened. The weather was perfect. It was 28 degrees outside, and overnight a fresh two inches of snow had fallen. We had never been up north bobcat hunting before, and we didn't know any of the area we were going to. The only reference we had was a county map, which designated rivers and streams. We knew that a river or stream would lead eventually to a cedar swamp, which in turn led us to where rabbits live. Snowshoe hare happens to be the main diet of the bobcat, with cottontail, mice, red, gray, and fox squirrels, plus other little rodents making up the rest. Strayed house cats are a favorite when they are available. If food is plentiful, the bobcat doesn't have to travel far for meals and can live in 40-80 acre area for the winter. On the other hand, if food is scarce, a bobcat will travel many more miles looking for a meal. It was for one of these wanderers we were looking.

This was something new for both of us. We didn't have real 'cat' dogs, but we did have 'coon' dogs, which had treed house cats. Dusty, my two and a half year old Bluetick who had been born the runt of the litter, with one eye, was small and didn't sell, so I had kept her. She treed 14 coons when she was just 6 months old. She had become a super hard tree dog on coon, and hated house cats. She had treed 6 or 7 house cats while coon hunting at night, so we decided to try her on bobcat. Buck, the other Bluetick, was one and a half years old, and I had just sold him to Bob. I had tried to get him started on coon at 6 months, but he wouldn't even look sideways at one. So I just didn't hunt him much for the first kill season. The following spring, I set my live trap to catch coon, but caught a big, old cat instead. He just looked at that cat and stood there, wagging his tail. I let the cat loose, letting it get just out of sight, then I released Buck. He ran the cat for about 600 yards, and then there was nothing. Only silence. I began to think he would never tree when I heard him making the loudest racket I'd ever heard him make. He had treed his first critter. From then on, he treed every house cat around! Sometimes I heard him tree for us to 20-30 minutes before I could get to him. He hunted well by the next fall, and was starting to turn into a good dog. Bob and I decided that we had our 'cat' dogs for our cat-hunting trip.

We had driven for 2 miles down the two-track until we came to a cedar swamp. Deer tracks laced the road in both directions. There were so many, and just when we began to get sick of checking to see what they were, I spotted a fresh track leading right down the road, then out into the swamp. I hollered to Bob, "Cat tracks! Stop the truck!" We stopped, and checked the tracks. They were perfect cat tracks. We could still see the pad marks in the bottom of the tracks. This being our first time at 'cat' hunting, we weren't sure how to start the dogs. We finally decided to keep the dogs on a leash until they opened on the track.

Bob carried a .22 rifle, while I carried a .16 gauge shotgun and a .22 revolver. We had heard that sometimes these cats would run circles and not tree. So we brought the shotgun.

As we led the dogs through the swamp, the going was very rough. Because a recent thaw had melted the ice bogs, with every three or four steps we took, we sank to our knees. We had to grab trees to get ourselves out, but we continued on for about 200 yards.

The dogs were interested in the track, but wouldn't open. They stuck their noses down deep in the track and took a good deep whiff, but it wasn't warm enough for them to open on. We went deeper into the swamp, sinking into the bogs, sweating, and just beginning just plain frustrated, with our dogs pulling on the leashes the whole time. We came to a big log and finally sat for a minute. We decided to let Dusty loose and hoped she would go on and 'jump' the cat. As we continued into the swamp, I was freed, but Bob was still tethered to his hound. We kept going deeper, Dusty went on ahead, but never opened. She got about 50 yards ahead of us when I heard her open with just a couple of barks. I hollered to Bob, "Cut that pup loose!" Buck ran on ahead of us to Dusty and what we heard next was two Blueticks hammering on a tree. We looked at each other and headed to the tree.

Upon hearing the spot, Bob hollered back at me, "I see the cat, and it's a HUGE one!" I then saw it too. About 20 yards ahead, high in a dead pine tree, there against the sky was what looked to be a huge bobcat, glowering down on the howling, treeing dogs. We moved closer, and as we did, our huge cat turned out to be two huge boar coon, one on one side of the tree, and one on the other side of the tree. The two coons wrapped around that tree had looked exactly like a huge cat from a short distance away. Cat on the brain could've influenced our judgment a little though. We got to the tree, and Bob just shook his head and said, "We drive all the way up here, to hunt cats, and they tree coons." Jokingly, he snickered a little and said, "All we have is trash hounds!"

I just smiled to myself as I looked at those two hounds shaking that tree. Deep down, I knew that he was just as proud as I was of those 'cat' dogs.

Home Ground

Walking to my deer stand one night, I came to a sandy area on a side hill. "The foxes must have a den here," I thought, noticing fresh sand thrown out.

Boom! My feet went out from under me, and down I went! The ground gave way to a big hole. The light went out. I was in a huge hole underground. I turned my flashlight on as the dust was settling. I was in an underground network of tunnels.

"So this is where they live," I said to myself. Off to one side was a sign over a hole, which read, 'Raccoon Lair.' To my right was 'Badger Bay' Down the tunnel was 'Woodchuck Castle,' 'Fox's Den,' 'Possum Lodge,' and on and on it went.

"So this is why I never see them," I said to myself. "They live underground in their own world." The tunnels twisted around and around until I saw a light ahead. I walked on to the light, which led me to a hole under a big oak tree. I walked out into the woods, then on to my deer stand.

~Grandpa

Thank You Lady

Lady finally opened on the track. I knew I might as well load my gun and head for the tree. The coon was either going to climb, hole up, or Lady was going to catch it on the ground!

The critter's squalling cry from the swamp helped me pinpoint their location. As I hurried through the woods, I could hear the sounds of the fight between them. Lady was and old Bluetick, and I knew she could handle herself one on one with a coon on dry land, but I was worried because I didn't know how deep the water was. I knew they were in the water for I heard the splashing during the fight.

I busted the brush to get to them, but I found that the swamp water was only 8-10" deep.

Lady had the advantage in their fight. That coon was gasping its last breath as my dog clamped her vise like jaws on its chest.

As I splashed over to her, she slowly wagged her tail until the coon stopped breathing. She then dropped the coon and the fight was over.

I had bought Lady from an old hillbilly who couldn't hunt anymore. "You can try her out," he said to me, "but I know that you'll like her."

I tried her out for a couple of nights and found that he was right. She was a good, fun dog to hunt. She wasn't a mouthy dog, and didn't run trash. She was also a super tree dog. Like I said before, if she barked on track, load up your gun!

I'd killed a lot of coon with Pete and Lady. Pete was a young, mouthy Bluetick who loved to run track. Lady tolerated him, but she was the power dog and the tree dog. Lady was a complete hunter without Pete. But Pete wasn't a complete coon dog without Lady.

The man had trained Lady to come to him when he called. She obeyed, no matter where she was. When called, she came and walked out of the woods at your side as the snap of a finer. I wish I could take credit for training her, but I can't, because I didn't.

She was a medium build hound with a gray back and light tan around the inside of her legs. She was a shy dog, and rarely ever barked on her chain. She was a dog whose bite was whose than her bark. I never had a kill dog like her. When a coon hit the ground, she didn't grab it by the behind, just barking and growling. She always dove right to the chest and clamped down with her vise-like jaws.

"Lady, it was fun hunting with you. Thanks for the memories."

Borrowed Shanty

My son Dave had built a small spearing shanty, which was sitting in the garage. "Dave are you going to use that shanty or not?" I asked him. "If you're not, do you mind if I set it up so we can both use it?"

"If you want to set it up that's okay with me," he answered.

I loaded the shanty onto his truck and we headed for the river backwater in Middleville. We drove down the railroad track and slid it down the bank into the ice.

The dam had been out for a few years now. The water level was low but deep enough for spearing.

I cut my hole in the ice, slid my shanty over the hole, and then crawled into the shanty. The bottom was black, so I dropped some corn onto the bottom. I could see now, for I was only in 2.5 foot of water. This wasn't as deep as I wanted, but it would do. I dropped my sucker minnow decoy into the hole, then pulled him about off the bottom. I was ready.

My decoy started going nuts. Something was making him nervous. The pike came in so fast it made me jump. A huge lunging fish in that shallow water would startle anybody. He lunged at the decoy, but missed. I got my spear ready for his next pass. He turned and came back but I was ready. I nailed a nice 30" northern behind the head. I flipped that one onto the ice and waited for more. I speared 3 nice pike that afternoon.

I drove home eager to show my catch. "Dave, I initiated your shanty today. 3 pike on her first outing."

The sad part of the story is Dave never got to use his shanty. We got a quick warm-up and the shanty went down when the ice got bad.

Dogs that Were

I was laid off from construction work, and was living in the wooded hills of Middleville. I had plenty of time for drinking coffee and staring out of the window in the mornings. One winter day, I noticed two black dogs running deer. There was lots of snow, so the dogs could push the deer hard. They would come through at the same time every day. One morning, as they crossed the backfield, I grabbed my .22 and fired a shot over their heads. They vanished. I did this a couple of days in a row, and it wasn't long before they wised up on me. They continued running the deer just beyond sight of the house. I knew one of them has to go, because just one dog usually wouldn't bother the deer. But if a pack got started, they could really ravage the deer.

I was drinking coffee one morning when I saw them sneaking through the brush. I grabbed my deer rifle, hoping to head them off. I went back to a clear area and watched for them. They ran the deer in silence, so I didn't know where they were, but I was hoping they'd come through the clearing.

As I stood in the snow, waiting, nature called, and it wasn't the standing kind if you know what I mean. I had paper in my pocket. As I squatted down, there they came, sneaking through the clearing. I grabbed my rifle and dropped the lead dog. I never saw the other dog again.

There are some people who think their dogs are perfect. You call them up, and they say, "Are you sure that's my dog?"

A friend of mine, called Stub, told me a story of two dogs. His dad, brothers, and himself would ride a sleigh to school. The neighbor's dogs would come out and harass the horses and the boys. Their dad, Buck, called up the neighbor who owned the dogs.

"Curly," he said, "your dogs are bothering my boys on the way to school."

"Are you sure those are my dogs?" Curly asked. "My dogs never leave the yard."

"Yeah," said Buck, "those are your dogs alright."

The dogs continued to harass the boys and the horses as they passed every day. So Buck gave the boys a pistol and told them, "If those dogs bother you again, shoot them."

The next morning, the dogs came out as usual. The boys shot two shots off at close range. Two dogs lay dead. The boys let them lay and went to school. The next day, Curly called Buck.

"Buck, have you seen my dogs?"

"No," Buck answered, "I haven't seen your dogs. My boys shot two troublemakers the other day, but they couldn't have been yours; your dogs never leave the yard!"

When someone calls you to tell you your dog is causing trouble, check it out! Dogs are a lot like children, you can train them, but they will make mistakes.

Busted

The game warden stood in the middle of trail motioning me to stop. I had finished pheasant hunting, and was driving out to the main road, and there he was!

I pulled over and rolled my window down.

"Get any birds Dave?" he asked.

"Yeah, I got a couple."

"I'd like to see them," he said.

The warden was Russel Rounds, a friend of the family. My dad always said, "Russel is a fair man, but there's no gray areas, it's either right, or wrong."

I had been hunting pheasants on state land. The DNR was trying a new program called put and take. The state raised the birds, then put them on state land for hunters to take.

I had hunted the open fields for a half hour with my bird dog Penney. I hadn't seen a bird until I came to a locust grove. There were 3 roosters running along the edge. My dog was in an open field working toward these trees. The birds heard her but hadn't seen me.

The limit was 2 birds. After placing the 3 birds in my game pouch, I hurried back to my car.

I was driving a Volkswagen Beetle. The front hood held the spare tire. I placed the "extra" bird under the spare tire, then closed the hood.

"Sure you can see my birds Russ," I said, turning the car off. I reached behind the front seat, grabbed my game pouch and then showed him the birds.

"Nice fat birds," he said, "Should be good eating."

"Sure enough," I said. "See you later."

As I drove off, my thoughts went back to the hunt.

Penny has busted the brush behind the birds, they ran toward me, with Penney hot on their trail. The birds then ran on an angle away from me. I had seen they weren't going to fly. They were runners.

They probably couldn't fly, for they were pen raised, fat birds, and had been placed on state land the day before.

I had shot, and one bird tipped over. The others ran. I shot again, the other two flipped over. I had shot twice, and three birds lay dead.

As I continued driving down the road, I thought back to another time the old game warden had let me off. I had just lost my black lab the season before, and I was trying out a new bird dog.

I knew where some good coveys of woodcock had gathered. I took this new dog to a low area where she flushed several birds, which I shot.

Taking the birds home, I cleaned them, then left them soaking in a bowl of salt water.

Russel used to stop by our house to visit with my wife. He got along good with her, and she with him. He stopped one day as he was out picking artichoke roots. They talked for a while, then the talk turned to me.

"How's Dave doing?" he asked.

"Oh, Dave's doing great," my wife said. "He got a new dog this week and tried him out." She got the bowl of woodcock to show him the birds.

He looked them over, then turned to her and said very nicely, "Those are find birds, but you tell Dave that bird season doesn't open until next week."

I waved to Russ as I drove out onto the tar road.

Oh Russ if you knew what I had in my trunk, you wouldn't be smiling.

A Good Hunt

Driving to his deer stand he reflected on breakfast at the diner. Tim met Dewey and Bill and they'd talked about climbing into their tree stands in the dark.

"The wet, snowy, branches will be slippery," Dewey said. "Did you know that John died this year, falling from his tree?"

Bill said, "I think I'll wait till daylight to climb."

Following his flashlight beam to the tree, Tim decided to climb. He carefully climbed the big oak, which overlooked several deer tracks in a funnel area.

Small strips of dry land, which weaved through several water swamps, created the funnel. The bark of the small trees had been shredded. Several bucks had been using the tunnel routes.

He nestled into his crow's nest, and waited for morning light. The turkeys moved first, rustling through the swamp as they came off their morning roosts. A small putt putt, then a loud gobble. They made quite a racket as they moved through the swamp. His eyes caught a movement to the right. A deer was sneaking along a trail.

Was it a buck? He couldn't see antlers, but its head was down, trailing scent, like a buck would. The darkness prevented a good look, and the deer melted into the brush.

The morning was uneventful except for the sound of turkeys moving from swamp to swamp. A flock of crows had found a hawk atop a tree. They chased him from tree to tree, then they were gone. A doe and fawn slipped through on a trail, then they were gone.

He waited until 1 o'clock before climbing down. Quietly, he walked up a small draw for he knew deer bedded on the ridge ahead. The earlier snowfall had now melted, making the woods silent for walking. He watched a small doe on a side hill. The wind was in his face. She didn't know he was there. She moved to the bedding area with a big doe following her.

He let them move up the hill before moving on. Walking slowly and walking carefully, he saw them on the ridge ahead. The fawn ran ahead but the doe stood still looking over her shoulder.

A large gray body ran to her from the brush. What was it? A buck? It could be a buck, but he couldn't see its head! He moved for a better look when the deer caught his movement and ran off, their white flags held high.

He never fired a shot that morning, but he had his best hunt ever.

Pat in Snow

I woke finding we had a heavy snowfall during the night. The fluffy 10" of snow laid heavy on all the shrubs and tree branches. I hadn't hunted pats in the snow during the late season in years. I ate a quick breakfast then headed out, remembering a couple of good spots I wanted to hunt.

Ruffed grouse "pats" burrow down into the snow to conserve heat. Then they bust out when a predator comes too close.

The snowy landscape looked void of any animal life. Looking closer, I could see the tracks of the night. The deer, fox, and rabbits had been out.

I walked slowly in the soft powder snow. The sun warmed the branches and puffs of snow fell around me.

I slowly circled a button bush swamp when from the snow three pats burst out from their snowy prison. I knocked one down but didn't have time for another shot.

I hit a couple more swamps taking a couple more pats. I missed many more. They'd burst from the snow right at my feet. I'd have shot many more if I hadn't been so startled.

Pike Dreams

My wife and I sat in the darkened spearing shanty staring at my huge sucker minnow swimming slowly then drifting back to the middle of the hole.

The day had begun with anticipation as usual. The dream of a big fish was half the fun of spearing.

My brother Phil, his wife Nancy and our friend Ade had all met for breakfast at a small restaurant in Newaygo. We'd heard of a small lake where big bluegill and lots of pike were there for the taking.

We'd had 12" of snow the night before so it was a job getting our shanties to the lake. We didn't take just one shanty to check out a new lake. We had to take all three.

Now here we were sitting and waiting. The work and anticipation was done. Now all we had to do was wait.

I whispered to my wife wondering if I'd bought too big a minnow. The 12" sucker looked huge swimming in that clean water. I wondered if there were any pike in that like that could take a minnow that size.

We sat watching and waiting for a couple of hours. She had to go to the bathroom, BAD! I opened the door letting her out and heard her walk toward shore.

She had gone about 30 yards when I saw it. A big pike was hanging just outside the hole. I had to lean sideways to see him. The huge eyes seemed glazed over as he stared my decoy down.

I was slowly getting my spear in position when he charged. I had no chance to throw. He grabbed that decoy peeled 20 yards off my reel then stopped. I figured he was turning the minnow to eat it.

The line started moving slowly. He was swimming away and the line was not whizzing through my fingers.

He stopped again then I started hand lining him back to my hole. He came back too easy, I was thinking. I grabbed my spear as I saw him come sliding back into the hole. He must have seen the spear coming as I threw it at him for he made one last lunge. The spear missed. The line cut through my fingers. The line actually ate my pinky finger to the bone. The leader snapped and the fight was over.

When my wife returned she found the shanty a mess. Line was all over and I was shaking. "What happened?" she asked.

I replied, "Let me tell you a story, but you probably won't believe it."

The First Shot

"You've got to try bow-hunting again," my brother said as he urged me to buy a bow. "It's a lot different now with compound bow and portable tree stands."

I had hunted with a recurve years earlier, lost interest, went back to bird hunting, then had coon dogs for the last ten years.

We stopped at an archery shop after work. They fitted my bow with arrows and a release. He was right; these new bows were faster and easier. Before I walked out of the shop I was shooting a nice grouping of arrows.

I felt a new excitement using my new bow. My son and I practiced nightly. I had found a new confidence in bowhunting.

I waited anxiously for the October 1st opener. The area I had scouted was riddled with buck rubs. I settled on a huge oak overlooking some runs next to a stream.

My nephews, Ryan and Adam, went up to our cabin the night before. We were ready.

Our stands were hung, and our gear was prepared. We drove around looking for deer. The deer were moving. We saw 10 does and 2 bucks.

Morning finally came. Rain and more rain! My young eager nephews were getting ready to go out. "You're going out in this downpour?" I asked.

"You bet," they said as they walked out the door.

The rain was falling harder as I fixed a cup of coffee, trying to decide on a wet tree stand or a warm bed. I was up here to hunt, so I headed out.

I sloshed back to my stand then climbed the wet slimy branches of the oak tree. I rested on my seat as the rain ran down my back. I was soaked in 10 minutes. The rain kept pouring down. I left after 20 minutes thinking this was stupid. I hate bowhunting. I walked back to the warm cabin.

My nephews returned all excited. Ryan had hit a buck but they couldn't find it. They were going back to look and wondered if I wanted to go.

We looked and looked for that buck but never found that deer. The rain had washed all the blood away.

We waited for the rain to quit, then I went scouting for a new spot to hunt. I found a huge beech tree next to a swamp where bucks had shredded the bark on the alders. I climbed the beech and found a perfect branch, the massive "arm" leaning back, just right for a backrest. It was like sitting in an easy chair.

I walked back for the evening hunt. I thought, "I'll try this one more time. I'll just sit back and enjoy God's creation. If I get a shot, then all the better."

After climbing the beech and getting my gear arranged I settled back and relaxed. The evening was beautiful. The sky had cleared birds were singing and the squirrels were everywhere gathering nuts.

I decided to try my grunt call. I'd never used one before and heard that you grunt three times, then wait half an hour, then grunt again. I did that for a while but I saw no deer. I tried louder, softer, more, less. Nothing was happening. I then relaxed, sat back, and decided to just enjoy the evening.

I heard something crack over to my left. I grunted a few more soft grunts then saw the body of a deer 35 yards away in some thick brush.

He moved through the brush, standing, looking, and moving slowly, finally stopping 40 yards away. My heart was pounding. This was the biggest buck I'd ever seen with a weapon in my hand.

He slowly turned his massive head around. He had at least 12 points with a 24" spread. Be still my heard. The beating was too loud.

He stayed out of bow range. I never got a shot, but what a way to get hooked on bow hunting! That was one of my most memorable hunts even though I never fired a shot.

First Fox

I cautiously approached the set. Everything looked different. The set was all torn up and a big mound of dirt was pilled up where my trap had been.

With great anticipation I had made the long walk to my set and mulled over the circumstances which had brought me to this point. I was 48 years old and had never caught a canine. I had water trapped for coon, mink, and rats for 15 years but never for fox or coyote.

My partner Sonny had invited me to fox trap with him, before we started our water line. I watched and learned as he made and remade sets. He taught me his main set, the dirt hole set. He dug a hole at an angle, with his trowel, then dabbed some lure on a cotton ball and shoved it into the bottom of the hole. Next, he staked the trap with two stakes. Double staking is necessary for there are large coyotes in our area. After staking he set the trap and bedded it firmly, so it didn't rock. Next he placed a baggie over the trap pan and sifted dirt over the trap, making sure the dirt was level and not mounded up. His final touch was a couple of shots of fox urine. "The secret," he told me, "is cleanliness." We boiled and waxed our traps, using clean traps whenever an animal had been caught. Clean cotton gloves were also changed often.

I knew of a good spot where I wanted to make a fox set. My destination led me on a long walk to a sandy area on state land. Fox had been digging ground squirrels and the area was all torn up.

I was satisfied with the set I'd made. I had finally done it! I walked back daily, checking and hoping, but caught nothing but a skunk.

One day after running our other line, I walked back to my set. Everything was different, all tore up! I thought I'd trapped a badger. I ran back to my truck and grabbed my .22. After returning to the site, I cautiously kicked at the mound of dirt, then taking a stick, I poked into the sand but nothing moved. After pulling the dirt away I uncovered a nice red fox that had gotten caught in the trap. Coyotes had found him, killed him, then covered him with a mound of sand. They had dug a ring around the edge one and a half feet deep, and covered the fox with a mound of loose sand!

I never caught another animal at this set. My first fox was killed by coyotes!

Do You Believe In?

Stepping out of the house, the moon was just rising over the trees. I had been coon-hunting for three weeks, and had decided to take the night off. "Sure is a beautiful night," I thought. "Nope, I'm staying home."

I heard dogs running in the distance. They were running deep in the section, rough country. They must have turned, I couldn't hear them anymore.

I walked up to check my dogs before I went in. Gleem, my old dog came out to greet me, then went back to her coop. She was tired. I walked to the pup's coops. They were gone! My mind raced to the dogs I had heard earlier. The pups! How had they gotten loose? I didn't know, but they were gone!

"I guess that I *am* going coon hunting tonight," I told my wife. "The pups are loose and are running back by Big Bear Swamp." I grabbed my light and gun, then headed out.

I hadn't charged my light but I thought I had enough battery to get to the dogs, if used sparingly.

The moon brightly lit the field as I walked across it. So as I made my way through the big woods, I used my light only as needed. The dog's voices were coming in clearer now.

I walked through a clear-cut, then over a ridge, which led to the swamp. The moon went under the clouds when I hit the ridge. I turned my light on low. I walked on. The dogs were treed now.

Walking atop the ridge, my light went out. My battery was dead! Suddenly, I was aware of something walking behind me. I moved. It moved. I stopped. It stopped. Something was following me. The hair on my neck stood up. I was scared. What was this, I thought? The dogs were treed ahead of me; it wasn't them.

I remembered another time, waking the dogs home one night. I had them leashed as we walked the road homeward. Seeing something dark shoot across the road, I didn't get a good look at whatever it was.

I led the dogs over to its track, then unleashed them. They walked on the track for 5 feet then turned back, tails between their legs. They had wanted nothing to do with that track. The ridge I was walking was in line with the spot I'd seen the "Thing" cross the road.

I frantically reached into my pocket for my lighter. Following the dim glow, I hurried towards my dogs. The closer I got the better I felt. Finally, I made it to the dogs. I was so glad to see them.

I never heard the thing after that. I didn't know what was following me then, and I still don't, but the thing is still out there. I know he is. Make sure you have a good light when you go out at night.

City Coon Hunt

"I don't hear the dogs, do you?" I asked Sonny.

"No," he answered. "Sounds like they disappeared into thin air."

My friend Sonny and I were coon hunting together in the fall of 1985. The fur prices were high, and the woods were full of hunters. It seemed wherever you turned the dogs out, there was someone else hunting, or had been. We were having a hard time starting a coon, let alone treeing one.

Sonny was hunting a 6-year-old black and tan male named Joe. He was a small hot nosed dog and a good tree dog. We knew that when Joe bared, the coon was going up, or was already up, the tree.

I was hunting a 7-year-old Bluetick female named Gleem. She was cold nosed, but also a good tree dog. We were hunting our best dogs because we planned on hunting 'til morning.

We unloaded the dogs in one of our favorite spots, "the flats." This is an area of river bottom land, outside the village limits of Middleville, Michigan. We had always started coon in this mecca mixed with corn, soybeans and hardwoods with a river running through it.

Gleem struck a track first with a long bawl, then another. She was working a cold track but was slowly warming it up. We listened for a few minutes, then Sonny said, "See if you can get her off that track. It sounds like a rough track." He wanted some quick "pop-up" coon. Then both dogs joined in the race as their voices carried through the night air telling us the "race was on!"

The "race" was heading straight towards town. We hurried along, hoping the coon would tree soon, as the dogs were pushing hard now. As quick as the "race" began, it ended. The dogs sounded as though they had dropped into a hole. Nothing!

We ran to the river's edge to where we had last heard the dogs, looking and hoping. Sonny ran to the dam thinking that they had gotten tangled up there. I sat on the silent bank listening when I heard the faint bark of a dog.

I ran to the spot where the barking sounded like it was coming from the ground. The barking was coming from a 10" cement storm tile.

I knelt down and shone my light into the culvert. In the light, I saw my big Bluetick stuck in the pipe. She was about 75' into the pipe, on her belly, her front legs stretched out to the front, with her rear legs stretched out behind her. She was still trying to go forward, barking as hard as she could.

I shouted her name, trying to coax her out. The thunder rumbling in the distance made me increase my calling. I couldn't imagine a thunderstorm with our dogs caught in the storm sewer.

She finally started backing up, inch by inch, until she was out. After Gleem cleared the tile, I could hear Joe, who was smaller, still running the coon through the tile. The rain was quickly changing from a sprinkle to a larger splatter.

I hollered to Sonny that his dog was in the tile. He ran to the next street and pulled the grate, just as Joe was going through. Sonny ran to the next block, he pulled the grate, and grabbed his dog, just as Joe was trying to decide which of the four tiles the coon had gone through.

We decided that this was the first and last time that we could go 'city hunting.' We were happy to have our dogs back in the dogbox before the storm sewer filled. The rain was falling much harder now.

So Close Yet So Far Away

The small spike whitetail nervously stared into the brushy thicket, as the sun began to rise. A larger buck walked out from the brush, then charged, running the spike out from his territory. The buck wasn't huge and looked a lot like the buck I had shot at a month and a half earlier, with my bow.

Earlier, during bow hunting, I had been scouting for a new spot to hunt, and had found a huge maple overlooking a cattail swamp. This is where I hung my treestand.

I had climbed up hoping the rain would stop altogether. The hard rain earlier was letting up now, but the leaves continued to drip as a light drizzle came down. I settled into my seat and must have been a little too comfortable and dozed off for a few minutes. When I opened my eyes, a nice buck was walking through a clearing in the cattails. I drew on him and released my arrow. After I shot he disappeared. I waited for 20 minutes then climbed down to look for blood. I hunted till dark but found no blood or arrow. I had heard a loud smack when I'd shot and thought I'd hit a tree. I went back the next day and hunted for my arrow but never found a thing.

Now as I fired my shotgun this buck dropped in his tracks. As my brother Jim and I were hanging our bucks on the buckpole, I noticed something shiny in my deer's chest cavity. "Look at this," I said. "That's my broadhead in his spine." The broadhead was lodged in the vertebrae bone, if it had been one quarter of an inch to the right, it would have smashed between the vertebraes, a quarter inch up, it would have severed the spinal column, an inch and a half down it would have cut through both lungs. So close yet so far away!

After my wife and I butchered my deer, I took some parts to be ground. The butcher had a pile of broadheads on his table by the door. I remarked to him that a lot of deer had been arrowed. He replied, "That's nothing. I've thrown that many away already."

A word of caution to all deer hunters young and old. Bowhunting takes more and more deer. Be CAREFUL when field dressing your deer. A broadhead lodged in the chest cavity can slice your finger wide open, with or without gloves.

One More Coon

The coon pulled at the trap, trying to free itself as I motored up to the bank. "Who's trapping this stretch of river besides us?" I wondered.

We had a good trapping season. We had floated 27 miles of river, taking our share of coon, mink, and rats. We had fox trapped, road trapped, and trapped the river. We were sick of coon. There were days that we had skinned 50 coon. The coon skinning was over.

My partner, Sonny, had gone back to work. I was going to muskrat trap on the backwater. We had noticed many houses and feed beds, but didn't have time to trap them. I know had time and was going to pleasure trap this backwater area.

I loaded my boat with traps and stakes then set the first area of the marsh. I motored under the first bridge then remembered a little cove up river. I then noticed the coon.

I went over to it to dispatch the coon. Checking the trap also to find out who was trapping our river. I found my name on the tag. I took the coon back to the fur shed that night.

"I got another coon today," I told Sonny.

"Oh yeah?" he replied.

When I told him where I had taken the coon, he remembered the set.

"I pulled that section of river," he said. "That's okay, go ahead and skin it anyway."

That's Deer Hunting

I began this deer hunting season on October 1st. I hurried home, climbed the maple tree to my stand. I was hunting on my neighbor's property. The maple tree sits in a small grove of trees surrounded by fields with a few apple trees intermingled.

I've never been 'skunked' in this stand as far as seeing deer. I've missed more deer than I've gotten, but that's deer hunting.

As the darkness fell, a deer loped through the open field, too far for a bow shot. Then my eye caught a movement. A deer was sneaking its way along the edge of the field slowly working my way. I watched as it came toward me, nibbling here and there, walking, stopping, looking. I watched as the darkness slowly enveloped the deer. The hunt was over.

The next time I went out, I hunted with my brothers, Phil and Jim. It was opening weekend, but the weather was nasty, cold, windy, and rainy. Not nice for hunting but the fire in the cabin sure felt good. During the morning hunt, I sat in someone else's stand. I didn't feel good in this stand. I didn't see any deer, so I hung my own stand in a small cherry tree, next to a small clearing.

The rain let up in the afternoon so we headed out to try the evening hunt. The wind was blowing so hard, I thought the deer would not be moving, but I climbed anyway.

The wind swayed the small tree back and forth. "Boy, this is like a carnival ride," I thought to myself. "I'm never going to hold still for a shot." Then the rain came. Wet, soaking rain. Finally it stopped and the wind let up.

Off to my right I heard something. A deer? I hadn't heard anything with the wind and rain. I turned slowly to my right. "The worst possible place for a shot," I thought. Two deer stepped from the brush then slowly walked towards me. There was a fawn behind a big doe, who was spooked from the wind. I waited to draw my bow until the doe was behind some brush and the fawn's head was turned. I had four eyes watching for movement. I held my bow, waiting for her to step out. She just stood there, looking and watching. She stood, and stood. Finally, my arms were so tired, I had to shoot, or let my draw off. I leaned ahead, saw a small opening, and fired my arrow. I missed over her back, but I had fun watching those deer that close.

The next time I hunted, I sat in a tree stand on our fence line up north. We had an early gun season for does up here.

The sun lit the field as the day began. A slight breeze from the southwest. Perfect! The deer wouldn't smell me as they moved to the swamp to hide during daylight.

Four deer slowly browsed their way across the field. I was too far for a shot. A truck bounced down the road. It was a perfect distraction. I climbed down the tree. They didn't see me. I crawled through the tall goldenrod towards the deer with the wind in my face. They couldn't see me. I couldn't see them.

I crawled along peeking up over the tall weeds. I couldn't see anything. But wait! There was a deer 75 yards ahead. I kneeled, took aim, then fired. The deer ran off. I thought I had hit her so I walked slowly, looking for blood. No blood. I had missed. Feeling dejected, I drove to the house to have some breakfast. As I took my gun from the car to the house, my hand slipped along the barrel. My rear sight had flipped, and it had made my shot way low. Oh well, that's hunting.

~Grandpa

I'll Never Know

As the sun was rising, we slipped our boat into the water, trying not to disturb the morning stillness. It was a nice, warm, summer morning on the river. You never know what kind of fish you're going to hook into in a river.

My brother Slick smiled at me with his toothless grin. "Looks like a good day," he said. I nodded. We decided to spat surface lures along the river's edge.

We'd floated a quarter of a mile when the sunbeams penetrated through the morning mist. The world was waking up. The birds were singing, and so were the mosquitoes.

We floated until we came to a small feeder stream, which dumped its cold, clean water into the river. I switched to a hula popper, made a cast, then let the ripples die around the lure. The water exploded. A huge fish smacked my lure. I jerked hard, trying to set the hook. The fish came to the boat fast! I reeled hard.

The fish rolled his eyes in disgust as he came alongside the boat.

"Slick, get the net!" I hollered.

Slick looked at me like I was nuts. "The net?" he said. "Might net a good-sized bass, but that monster won't begin to fit."

"Slick, I need this fish." I hissed. "This is the biggest fish I've ever had this close to the boat. Slick, stick your hand down there, and see if you can grab his gill plates or eye sockets."

Slick flashed his toothless grin at me. "Are you nuts?" he said. "Did you see those teeth? They look like sharks teeth."

"Come on, trust me," I said.

The musky had had enough. He peeled the line off my reel as I watched helplessly. He surfaced, tailwalking the surface, shook his head, threw the lure, and it was over.

"Man, you didn't even help me," I cried.

"I couldn't have done anything," Slick answered.

I thought about it for a minute, then said, "Yeah, maybe you're right. He wasn't hooked good anyway."

But could he have? He could have. He could have tried grabbing his eye sockets and how about the gill plates? How about a rope noose around its tail, or a club? I guess I'll never know.

Safe Trapping

"You can't trap a river and hunt for deer at the same time," Sonny said. We were getting our gear ready to trap a 6 mile stretch of river.

"Why not?" I said. I knew it was rough work, but why couldn't we come back with a boatload of coon, plus a nice buck draped over the bow?

We started setting traps on November 19th, four days after the opening of gun season. We figured that was plenty of time for things to cool down from the opener.

We slipped our 10' Jonboat into the water at daylight. We had it loaded with coil-spring traps, plus a big bucket of fish for bait. The whole picture looked good to me. We would have had plenty of room for a gun. We could've encased it and laid it on the middle seat, but decided against it.

I started the trip rowing from the back seat. We floated with the current and I basically steered us through the rough spots. Sonny sat in the bow pointing out the best spots to make our sets.

We made our sets as fast as possible. We used pocket sets under the roots of the big river trees. The trap setter sits on the front of the boat and points out the spots he wants to set. When we approached the bank, he jumps out, holds the boat, and makes a set. Taking a trowel he makes a hole, jabs some bait in, wires the trap to a root, sets the traps, and then we're off again. The oar man stays in the boat, stands up, then ties a ribbon to a branch to mark the set.

We had floated about halfway down the river. The day was beautiful everything was going good. We were making a set next to a 6' bank. Sonny got out to make the set as I marked the branch. As

I stood to tie the ribbon, I saw a buck jump up 10' from me. His front leg had been shot and he wasn't going good.

We tied the boat and watched as the buck stumbled into the brush.

"Grab the gun!" Sonny hollered.

"What gun? We didn't bring one, remember?"

We grabbed our trowels, and chased the wounded buck. We spent 10-15 minutes chasing him, but it's hard to shoot a deer with a trowel. As we walked back to the boat Sonny said, "We'd better take a gun tomorrow."

We floated down river surprising several does and one more buck. The load in the boat was getting lighter. The more traps we set, the more room we made. We would have plenty of room for a gun.

We met at the fur shed the next morning for coffee. "Well, how many coon are yankin'?" Sonny asked.

"I don't know, but I say we'll get 15 coon," I answered.

"The coon really ran last night," he said. "Did you bring a gun?"

"Yeah," I answered.

Excitedly, we drove to our starting point. This could be our day for a boatload of coon plus a nice buck.

We organized the boat before starting out all nice and neat. We floated to our first set.

"There he is!" Sonny hollered. "Do you see him?"

"I don't yet." I was in the back steering. He was in the front hollering and looking. We harvested that coon and twelve others by the time we got to the "wounded buck" set.

We were starting to take on some weight. The coon we'd caught were all nice and large. We had added another 200 pounds and we were making a mess of the boat.

Of course, as we had a gun today, we didn't see the buck at "wounded buck set."

We floated down river, adding more coon along the way. We now had 20 coon and our boat was scraping rocks. As we came around a bend, Sonny whispered, "A buck! Hand me the gun."

I slipped the gun out of the case and handed it to him. The buck was feeding and didn't see us. Sonny was standing up, aiming the gun.

"Just a little closer," he whispered. "Keep her straight."

I did my best but didn't see the shallows ahead. Sonny was readying to shoot when we hit the rocks.

The boat lurched as the buck ran off. He glared at me. "What was that all about?"

I just shrugged my shoulders and said, "Too many coon."

We had one more chance at a nice buck that day. He was at the bottom of a steep bank. He couldn't get up the bank but was too far for a shot.

Sonny cussed the coon. "If we didn't have these coon we could go faster."

We now had 25 coon. We couldn't pass through the shallows without getting out and pulling the boat. The buck moved when we moved, staying out of shotgun range. After we took a long shot, the buck ran out of sight.

"I am sick of these coon," Sonny said. "We could have had two nice bucks if it weren't for these coon."

"If it weren't for these coon we wouldn't be here," I said.

We were both thankful for the day. We harvested 30 coon that trip plus had the chance for two bucks.

Well now I see why you can't trap and deer hunt at the same time. A gun in a trapping boat is too dangerous. That was the last time we took a deer gun on our trapping floats. You can't trap a river and hut deer at the same time. I totally agree.

Needle in a Haystack

I had to find the needle but I knew it was hopeless. It had fallen into a pile of leaves, and there was no hope in finding it.

I had just begun coon hunting at age 35. Fur prices were good, good dogs were scarce, and very expensive.

I had tried out about 10 different dogs. The dogs I tried had run trash (deer, possum, and skunk), or they wouldn't tree. You need a good dog to catch coon. A dog that will run track, locate the tree, then hold the tree until you get there.

I had finally found a good tree dog. Buck was a three year old Redtick, a lazy dog, but loved to tree. I also hunted with Ambler, a two year old Bluetick. He was a goofy dog. He loved to run and track, but couldn't, or wouldn't, tree.

I was running these two dogs one September night. I wanted these two males to get used to each other before the season began October 1st.

I cut them loose on the edge of a gravel road. They headed for an oak ridge where the coon were feeding. Ambler struck first with his long bawl.

They ran for 20 minutes, then I heard Buck locate the tree with one long bawl then began hammering out his machine gun tree bark. They were treed so I headed towards the tree they had picked. I've heard people say, "I don't need a compass because I know these woods like the back of my hand." I knew these woods that good. I always pay attention to where I am going, and where I have been. I try to find my way without a compass, but always carry one.

I finally made my way to the huge oak tree full of leaves. I walked round and round, trying to locate the coon. I found them.

There was a whole litter of young coon. Their yellow eyes shone down at me, as I praised the dogs, leashed them, and then headed out.

I had lost my bearings going round and round the tree. I reached into my pocket for my compass. When I opened the compass case, I noticed the needle had fallen off the post. I made the dogs sit, so I could set the needle on the post, and get my bearings.

I had just set the needle back on the post when the dogs jumped up and jerked the leash. They must have heard something in the woods. When they jerked, my needle fell off my compass to the forest floor.

I looked for the needle for a few minutes, but it was hopeless. The night was black and the woods were big. The dogs wanted to hunt, and I wanted to go home.

I made my way out of the woods that night by shining my light on one tree which was straight ahead. I walked to this tree, then shined ahead to another, and another. I kept walking in a straight line from tree to tree until I made it to the road.

I was two miles from my truck, but I could walk that far as long as I knew where I was. I went out the next day, and bought a new compass.

Being lost in the woods that night reminds me of life. The dark woods are like our trouble around us. If we don't look at them, but just focus our light, which is Jesus, on His trail, soon, we are out to the road again.

Stay on Track

It was two o'clock in the morning. I wanted to go home but my dog was racing across an open field towards a barn. The last thing I wanted to do was wake a farmer at night!

My son, Todd, and his friend Curt, wanted to go coon hunting. We loaded the dogs in the dog-box, then headed for a swamp on Robertson road.

We were hunting Pete and Lady. Pete was a young dog, with no papers, but looked like a purebred Walker. He was a better strike dog, but he would tree.

Lady was an older Bluetick. She wasn't a mouthy dog, but when she opened you better get ready, for she was going to tree, or catch the coon on the ground.

Pete struck first. They were running together but Lady wasn't singing. They took the coon around the edge of the swamp then into the water. Lady finally opened and the race was on. They treed in a huge oak on a ridge and we took off for it. We had only been out for 15 minutes and the dogs had treed!

We shined our lights and found the coon. I took my 22 rifle off my back and began sliding shells down the tube. The dogs had learned, when they heard the shells being loaded into the gun, to be quiet. The shells meant the coon was coming down and they wanted to hear the coon hit the ground. We shot the coon out. It was a nice, big boar.

We loaded the dogs, and tried another spot. We hunted for one and a half hours but never treed again.

The boys were tired, and having school the next day, decided to call it quits. I took them home.

The time was 11:30 pm, but it was too early to quit because the coon were prime. I decided to try another woods, two miles to the east. I tied Pete up, and loaded Lady.

I unloaded Lady, then headed to the woods. I thought I might catch a few lay-up coon. Lay-up coon are coon which have fed earlier in the evening, then climb a big tree, and sprawl out on a limb waiting for their food to digest.

Lady worked the big woods, hunting and checking. She was always a little mouthier when running alone. She finally struck a track.

She worked it through the woods then hit an open field. Lady had never run deer before but there's always a first time. She ran across the field to a small slope, then back into the field, smokin' the track. I was worried because I heard her turn and head straight for the barn.

I thought, "This is great, she's going to 'tree' in that barn." I should have quit with the boys. She was heading for the barn when I heard her locate, then tree.

I looked into the field wondering what she had treed on. I couldn't see anything. I turned my light on, then headed towards her barking. I could make out a small stand of trees ahead of me. As I walked up, I saw she had treed three large coon in one small tree.

Three shots later, I was admiring three large boars lying on the ground. I was happy I hadn't quit earlier. I was also happy Lady knew what she was doing. She wouldn't have treed those coon if she had listened to me when I had tried to call her off the track as she as running in the open field.

There is a time when we have to do what is right, what we have been taught, and trained to do even though others may try to persuade us off the track.

Ice Spearing

"Throw me the rope!" I hollered. I was up to my waist in ice cold water, and I wanted out.

My brother Jim, my friend Sonny, and I were laid off the winter of 1988. It was January and ice spearing season was open. Until now, we hadn't much cold weather to make good ice, but the previous few nights had been in the teens. This was cold enough to finally make good ice so we headed to the blackwater of the Thornapple River in Middleville.

We walked onto the ice, spuds in hand checking the ice as we went. It held good. There was one and a half to two inches of good, clear, hard ice. It was so crystal clear you could see the bottom as we walked across. We saw several different kinds of fish swimming below us. Among them were large dogfish cruising for a meal.

We walked quietly until we saw a big 'dogger' ahead of us. Then ran to the fish, trying to stun them with our spuds.

We decided the ice was hard enough to set up for spearing. Sonny had a fold-up tent Jim and I had portable wood shanties, which we set and waited for action. We had speared a few dogfish when I noticed a little water on top of the ice inside my shanty. The day was warm and sunny, and the black-muck bottom was pulling the sun's warmth toward it. I sat watching for fish noticing more and more water.

The combined weight of the shanty, and myself, caused the ice to bend. The more the ice bent, the more water sat on top. I was going to go down! I had to get out of there.

I opened the door, and scrambled out just as the shanty went down. The ice had buckled with all the weight. Fortunately, the black water was only 2 feet deep, but I was still up to my waist in water, and up to my knees in muck.

I hollered for help, but all I got was laughter. Sonny and Jim were lighter than I, and suggested I lose some weight.

They finally threw me the rope. They pulled and pulled until I finally slithered onto firm ice. Sonny and Jim were still laughing as I struggled to the truck. My clothes were beginning to freeze and I had to get warm.

Kim

We got Kim as a Pup when I was 12 years old. My dad brought home another pup a few weeks earlier, but he had to get rid of it because it became sick with distemper. A few days later, he brought home this other little squirt. It acted like an older dog, even as a pup. He was smart and acted smart.

He looked like a miniature black and tan with its tail curled up over its back. He had shorter legs and an aloof, confident attitude for something so small!

My brothers and sisters began suggesting names for him, but I had the final privilege of naming him. We decided on Kim, after a Korean orphan that my folks had sponsored.

Kim looked a little bit like a dachshund, so we looked up "dachshund" in the World Book Encyclopedia. This dog was used for digging badgers from their dens. We thought we had a "hole" dog, and we decided to find out!

We found a rabbit hole, and began training him. Kim didn't want to go down in the opening so we shoved him down, head first. Then my brother Phil sat on top of the hole. My brother Jim and I would go to the connecting hole and call Kim's name. After a while, Kim made it through to the other end, and we knew for sure that we had a "hole" dog!

We began Kim's rabbit training in our basement in Caledonia, Michigan. Having stacks of old wooden chairs; we arranged them to make a maze. We then took our tame rabbits and let them run the "jungle" we had made. We let Kim loose at the same spot that we had released the rabbits. He began whimpering and yipping through our "jungle", with the rabbit staying just ahead. We know also had a rabbit dog!

Kim was the kind of dog that seemed to just know what you were hunting, whether it was a pheasant, rabbit, or coon. They all seemed to be his game.

When I was 14, my uncle Harm invited me to go pheasant hunting with him. Kim was 2 years old, and neither one of us had hunted pheasant before. Uncle Harm picked me up and on the way, asked me if Kim hunted pheasant. "I don't know, but he sure runs rabbits, he'll run pheasants." We took him out and Kim put up a nice big rooster, which Uncle Harm shot. We has us a pheasant dog now, too.

We never used Kim as a deer dog, because it is illegal to hunt deer with a dog in Michigan. Kim could run deer slow enough to allow for a good shot and if we had lived in the south, we would have had a good deer dog.

Later, we moved from Grand Rapids, Michigan to Gibson, a small town south of Holland, Michigan. My dad had a small church there, which came with plenty of extra acreage, making plenty of ground for us boys to roam in.

My buddy Jack would come out to spend the weekend with us once in a while. We would hunt and just goof around together with Kim. One day the four of us went rabbit hunting across from our home. We had hunted for a couple of hours when we heard Kim's voice change. He sounded like he was a mile away. We ran over to the spot that we had last heard him, thinking he had fallen into an old well or something. Instead, we found him in a hole deep in the ground. We tried coaxing him out, but he kept going deeper and deeper, until his voice faded completely out of hearing. We wondered what to do. Phil ran home and got a shovel, then we began digging out the entrance of the hole, which, when opened up, revealed an underground creek. We decided to lower Phil down, armed with a flashlight, and a pistol. Our friend had bought a pistol out west and usually carried it when we were hunting. In a while, Phil came back to the mouth of the hole. He told us that Kim had a big coon cornered in an underground cave, and wondered if he should shoot it. We told him to get as close as possible, and then shoot the coon in the mouth as it snarled. We heard two shots, some snarling and growling, then all was quiet. Phil came back and delivered us the big coon, then Kim. The coon was a big boar, weighing 25 pounds. We now had a coon dog.

When we lived in Gibson, I worked for a builder who loved to hunt. Anytime the weather was too bad to work, we would go hunting. He had a nice farm with huge weed fields that were great for pheasant. One drizzly afternoon, I took Kim out to these fields. After bagging one pheasant, Kim was hot on the trail of another. He flushed that rooster, and I shot, knocking the bird down. Marking the bird, Kim started tracking that crip. He kept going, and going and going. As he was heading back to the barns, I wondered if he was tracking a barn cat, but I kept following. He went right into the barnyard to a pile of horse manure, circled it, then climbed to the top. He started digging, then grabbed at something. The crippled rooster had buried himself in the manure, but Kim had found him! On the way home, the rooster we had gotten from the manure pile came back to life. Imagine driving a Volkswagen with a pheasant running under the seats, and a dog trying to get at him! I had to pull over to the side of the road, and put that pheasant out for good.

Kim lived for fifteen years, and then my mother had him put to sleep. He was a loyal friend and companion. He helped raise three young men. Thank you Kim for all the years and years of memories.

Spring Peepers

My coon-hunting partner for a few years was Bob Graham, who lived in the city. Bob always hunted three or four dogs so when I took my two we had a pack.

Bob had an old Bluetick named Belle that loved to hunt. She was a bullheaded trash running Bluetick, but she could also run and tree a coon. I think she would run deer then hit a hot coon track, switch to coon, then run and tree it.

I was hunting Buck, a three-year-old red-tick and Ambler a two-year-old Bluetick. Ambler was an idiot dog who'd run, track, but wouldn't tree.

We were training our dogs one spring night. The dogs hit a track and were all running together. The hound's music was running through the hills.

The dogs had moved on so we followed and came to a small pond.

The spring peepers were singing. They were so loud we couldn't hear the dogs. Bob had never heard spring peepers before and turned to me to ask, "What in the world is that noise?"

I told him spring peepers.

"Well," he said, "I've never heard that before, but it sure is loud. Come on, let's go find our dogs."

Penny

I got Penny when she was six months old. She was already 'trained.' A pretty dog, she looked like a small Irish Setter with light red, long, silky hair.

Penny was a whore of dogs. She was a tramp of all tramps. Even though she was loved and treated well, she would climb up, over the chain link fence every day, and run off to all the neighbors.

We'd have to go find her just about every evening. She couldn't get enough attention, or hunting. She hunted with the neighbors as well as with me. I hunted her for three seasons, and killed a lot of birds with her on point.

I remember a big oak blow-down where I'd go hunting in the December pat season. We'd put as many as 10 birds at a time out of this tangle.

My first double on pats was with Penny. We were coming out to the woods edge when she went on point. The first bird broke cover. I shot. It went down. The other bird broke cover and I dropped that one also. She was a hard running bird dog, but I was young and I could run, so that didn't bother me.

In the mid 70's, we had a fairly good population of pheasant for the Middleville area. My brother, Phil, and I had a hunting contest. Even though I hunted with Penny, Phil won, 22 to 19, that year.

I enjoyed hunting with her, but a tramp is a tramp and she tramped out of our lives to a life of wandering. She just disappeared one day, never to return.

A Falling Out

I've often wondered if a coon dog could tree a deer. I've wondered, do they run deer, then change to coon to save them from a beating, or do they actually run a coon that far?

I started down a two track east of our house. My coon dogs Buck, Ambler, and Bonnie were in the dog-box in the back of the truck. Driving down a hill, I got to the bottom when all three dogs opened in the box. They wouldn't stop barking. I drove to the top of the hill, thinking they had just winded something and would stop, but they didn't. "I'm here, why not just dump them on the track?" I thought. I was apprehensive. Was it a coon, deer, or fox?

I opened the dog box and all three dogs raced to the stop where they had first opened. The dogs hit the track and took it south towards the state road. They ran the track so hard and hot, I thought maybe they were running deer. I didn't know as I rested on the tailgate and listened to the sweet music of the hounds.

Taking the track out of hearing, they turned and started coming back. Running on such a straight line, I knew they must have been running deer. Pushing hard and fast, they were across the road before I could get there. The dogs pushed the track across a ridge then down into a swamp.

"Why would a deer head for a water swamp, thick with brush and button bushes?" I thought. As I headed for the swamp, I heard Buck locate on a tree with a long bawl. Suddenly, all three dogs were treeing. I was convinced the dogs had treed a deer, or had grabbed a tree to save them from a beating.

The night was cold and clear, in early November. The pale, sliver of a moon dimly lit the swamp. As I made my way to the tree, I saw it was on a small island in the middle of the swamp.

My headlight cut into the darkness as I ran toward the dogs, crashing through a half inch of shattering ice. I was amazed to see clouds of two inch pollywogs swimming beneath the surface of the clear ice. The dogs treed harder as they saw my light coming to them. I could see why. A huge coon was part way up, clinging to a dead tree.

The dogs had forced him to climb the first tree available! They were up on that tree so hard that it was shaking. I shot and dropped the coon. It was a nice 20 pound boar.

I was glad the dogs had treed, but I still didn't know if they have been running deer, and then switched to coon, or if that big boar had taken them on the run of their lives.

At the next spot that I turned the dogs out, they ran and treed in a matter of minutes. Walking to the tree, I felt good. Finally I had some dogs that could run and tree coon. I had spent all summer and fall trying to find good dogs. I had killed only a few coon earlier in the season. Suddenly, my tired legs didn't feel so tired.

Something was wrong as I walked to the tree. There was only one dog treeing. Where were the other two? Shining my light up the tree, I noticed the dogs had treed in a widow maker. A windstorm had tipped trees making a tangled mess of trees and vines. The area was 75x100 feet, and had a big tree leaning into the middle. I shone my light higher on the tree trying to locate the coon, when I noticed Buck walking on the leaner. He was 65 feet in the air. Calling to him gently. I tried to turn him. He stopped on the tree, trying to turn himself around. He wasn't a cat footed dog, but a large hound with big feet. He tried to turn, but couldn't. I felt a sick feeling in the pit of my stomach as he lost his balance, then fell to his death.

We had enjoyed a few weeks of good hunting, but now I had to find another dog. The other two dogs were worthless without Buck. HE WAS THE TREE DOG! I sadly rounded up Bonnie and Ambler, for I knew my season was finished!

Fawn on the Point

I woke early one warm summer morning to watch the day begin. The sun wasn't up yet as I walked out onto the deck. The wind was calm and the birds were just waking up. It was going to be a beautiful day.

My wife and I had a cup of coffee, then decided to go down to the lake and try some fishing.

We drove down the lane to the lake as the sun was rising. On the trail, close to the water, I saw something out of the corner of my eye. It was a big snapping turtle in the sand, looking for a spot to lay her eggs. The sand was crisscrossed with her tracks. She had dug several holes, which we checked. We found no eggs and continued on to the lake.

We fished off the dock on the main point for a while. The bluegills and sunfish were moving to their beds, but weren't biting at all. I got bored, so I decided to check the fishing on the other dock, around the point.

I had walked to a small haven that I had cut the week before. It was a grassy area on the very end of the peninsula, surrounded by a thicket. This waterside hedge consisted of tagalders/birch, ferns, and other brush.

Last summer I had walked this area early one morning and had seen a tiny fawn lying in the ferns.

Fishing pole in hand, I quietly walked into the opening, looking carefully for deer. Again, in the ferns, was another tiny newborn fawn. Its head was deep in the ferns and all I could see was its rear. He was standing, shaky and wobbly on his newborn legs. I quietly slipped back out, then ran to tell my wife what I had seen.

She said, "Oh, really? I just caught two bass!"

I decided to go back for another look.

I walked quietly into the haven, but didn't see anything. The redwing black-birds were screaming at me, because I was too close to their nest. I walked around looking for the fawn, and finally decided that he must be hidden, lying beneath the ferns. Oh, well it was a beautiful morning, and I HAD seen him once. Retracing my steps, I walked quietly back to the opening, and then I saw him again. He was laying under a fern. SO tiny, he looked no bigger than a housecat. He lay all balled up, and never moved a muscle!

I ran back, got my wife so that she could see it, TOO. We marveled at how tiny he was, and after a short while, left him.

Bullfrogs were croaking at the shore, leopard frogs were screaming in the field-marsh, and the crickets were chirping. The breeze felt great and we'd spent the morning enjoying all of it!

Lady

"Dad, I would feel better if we got out of here. That lady is probably going to call the police."

My son, Todd, and I were coon hunting my Uncle's farm. Surrounding the farm were big expensive houses. City slickers had bought their 5-10 acre parcels of land, then built their castle inside their sanctuary.

We had started hunting late in the evening, waiting for the castle owners to go to bed.

We cut our dogs loose deep in the section, hoping they'd stay away from the castles. We hunted for a couple of hours and caught a few coon.

Our dogs, Pete and Lady, started another track on the end of the woods. They lit out across an open field. We had a good race going. We were running a coon who was experienced at losing dogs. He was moving to his territory.

We crossed another open field then into a small woods. The dogs began hammering on the tree they'd found him in. "He's here. He's here. Over here," they said.

We walked to the tree, shining for the coon. The oak tree was huge. Its giant arms reaching to the top, were covered with leaves. "That big boy could be anywhere up there," I told Todd. The dogs kept hammering on the tree. We looked for 15 minutes, then I found him. A large coon up near the top.

I loaded my rifle, then shot. Thud. You could hear that it was a good hit. The coon moved higher into the leaves out of sight. "I hit him," I told Todd.

A light came on in one of the castles. We were treed in their backyard! A lady came to the back door and started screaming all sorts of obscenities. "Get out of here! I'm calling the law!"

I wanted that coon. The dogs had worked hard to find him, plus, I had wounded him. I was frustrated. I hollered back. "Shut up lady!"

We leashed the dogs, then headed for the road. We were walking on the black-top when Todd turned to me and said, "Dad, I am glad we have a dog named Lady."

"Why's that?"

"Well, if we get caught, you can explain that your dog's name is Lady, and you told her to shut up, then left."

We were walking toward our truck when a county cruiser pulled us over.

"We've had a complaint of coon hunters trespassing," he said. "Were you over on this property?"

"Yeah but we left when the lady screamed at us."

"The lady also reported that you told her to shut up," the officer said.

I explained our situation to him then told him that my dog's name was Lady. He got a smirk on his face, then said, "Well, you are not trespassing now. Have a good night boys."

Private Property

The spotlights searched the roadside while we laid on our dogs. We had to silence them. We didn't want the police to know our location.

We had started the night at the Jenk's farm. The pick-ups, loaded with coon dogs, had all pulled into the yard. We were to have a hunt, and the dogs knew it. Men unloaded dogs and tied them to trees, stakes, and truck bumpers. There were dogs everywhere. Excitement was in the air. We were having a club hunt with Morse Lake Coon Club. The club had 25-30 members, all waiting for darkness to fall so the hunt could begin.

The head hounds-man was dividing the hounds into different casts. The casts consisted of 3-4 dogs.

I walked to the head table to find out which cast I was in. We had a four-dog cast. Bugsy was hunting a 4 year-old Red Bone. Doc was hunting a 5 year-old Bluetick. His friend, Bud, whom I didn't know, was hunting a 4 year-old Bluetick. I was hunting Gleem, my 6 year-old Bluetick. We had drawn a good cast.

We drove to our hunting spot and unloaded our dogs. Doc had permission to hunt the land we were on. He told us he had permission on most areas around.

We unleashed our hounds and waited for them to start a track. Gleem opened first. I hope she isn't running trash, I thought, because no other dog opened. Doc's dog opened next, then all the dogs joined in. I breathed a sigh of relief.

The hounds were making sweet music as they pushed the track. The night was hot and still. Their voices carried well. We sat down, and listened to the race unfold. They crossed an open field into mature hardwoods. We moved up on the dogs. They ran a short distance, then treed. We didn't know which one treed first, for they had all treed together. They were hammering their 'treed.' The coon was up that tree!

We walked to the tree joking and laughing. We were all happy the dogs had run and treed together. A cast of strange dogs doesn't always work out that good. There are times when they fight, especially on the tree.

We got to the tree, then leashed our dogs, tying them to any branch, scrub, or small tree we could find. We shone our lights into the tree looking for the coon and found him. His eyes were blinking out at us from his leafy hideout. We were taking some pictures of the dogs when we noticed a pickup coming towards us.

We thought nothing of it as the truck neared, then stopped. A man got out, then walked over to us.

"What do you guys think you're doing?" he asked.

We told him we had a club hunt.

"Well, you're trespassing!" he hollered. It was then that we saw the pistol he waved over his head. "You are trespassing on my property and I called the law. They are on the way!"

We didn't argue with the pistol man, but did as he told us.

"I want you to move to my house. NOW!!!" he said.

We leashed our dogs and marched to his house. We tried to reason with him, but to no avail. His mind was made up.

When we arrived in his yard, he told us to put our dogs in his kennel.

"No way!!!" Doc and Bugsy argued with the man. "How would the law know those are our dogs? They'd be in your kennel."

While they were arguing with the man; Bud quietly drawled out of the corner of his mouth to me, "Don't say anything, just keep moving to the road."

We moved toward the road while the argument continued. We were halfway to the road when Pistol Man hollered at us to stop or he would shoot.

Bud in a whispered snarl said to me, "Let's go. Make a run for it."

We took off on a run, dragging our dogs with us. The man fired over our heads, but we had made it to the road.

Bud coughed and coughed when he caught me. "Slow down! We're safe now. There is nothing the law can do now that we are on the road. We're not trespassing."

We walked to our trucks then laid in the brush, waiting for Doc and Bugsy. Man! Were they mad when they found us! They had gotten a ticket for trespassing, and had to make a court appearance.

If you get caught trespassing, walk slowly towards the road while reasoning with the property owner, but don't be found on his property when the law arrives. God owns all property and, man has stewardship of His property. There are some people who think they own and control everything in God's creation.

You Never Know

"Don't worry Hon," I hollered as I walked out the door. "I'll be back in plenty of time for Thanksgiving dinner."

I had set 60 traps on the river the day before. The temps had warmed up during the night, and I just knew there would be fur in my traps. I had to run my trap line.

"You meet me at the first bridge at 10:30. That should give me plenty of time to run my line and still get to Todd's house for dinner."

I loaded my 8' pram, battery, and electric motor into the truck. I still needed my bait bucket, trowel, and pistol. I had loaded these final items when I thought about a paddle, in case the motor quit. I threw a paddle in, then drove to the river.

I slid the loaded boat in the water. The river level had risen a little during the night, but my first trap looked good. The water covered the top of the pan. We'd had a slow drizzle all night. "The coon must have really run," I thought to myself.

I motored past the first three sets; they looked good, but were empty. I was only rebaiting the sets I'd found with fur, in order to save time. I'd gone about a quarter of a mile when the rain started falling. I hadn't a raincoat, for the weatherman said no rain was to fall. I slipped the motor on high, and headed down river.

The rain started falling harder now. It was pouring! I could hardly see! I was soaked! BANG!!! I hit a log.

The motor snapped and quit. I monkeyed with it for a minute, then realized the wiring was messed up, and that I had no motor.

I thought about leaving the boat, walking to a house, and calling my wife, but the closest house was a mile away. I'd go on down river.

I grabbed the paddle, and started going, warming up with the work. I stopped to bail the boat because the rain was falling so hard. I thought back to a story my hunting partner, Sonny, had told me.

He had made 80 sets on the river, late in the season, when the temperatures were colder. He'd just started running his line when he hit a rock, upsetting his boat, throwing him into the frigid water. He climbed back into the boat and his soaked clothes froze instantly. He grabbed his oars, and started rowing to get warm. One oar broke. He grabbed the other oar, climbed up front, and paddled 2 miles like a mad dog. He warmed up enough by paddling to keep his clothes from freezing hard.

He made it to where his truck was parked. He jumped out, and ran to it. His keys were in his front pocket. His pants were frozen and froze harder as he struggled to get the keys. He managed to get them out and start his truck. He laid on the floor as the heater warmed his icy body.

I didn't have it as bad. At least it wasn't freezing out, but I was cold and wet. I paddled by my sets, hoping there wasn't any fur. I had to stop at 5 sets, and picked up 4 coon and a mink.

I finally made it to the bridge, and I was never so glad to see my wife in our car with the heater running. I was so glad I threw in that paddle. You Never Know!!!

Too Much Trouble?

We locked the front hubs of my 4 wheel drive. We had loaded my truck with shanties, sleds, toboggans, spears and minnow buckets. Our junk was crammed into every available spot.

This was January 1st, opening day for pike spearing. My brother Phil and I were going spearing. We knew we had a rough road ahead, for a lot of snow had fallen in December. We were going to Black Lake, by Middleville. The lake is bordered by woods on one edge, with fields on the other. We were coming in through the fields owned by Paul Palmer, who let us park in his yard while we fished.

After pulling into his yard, we unloaded our gear. Paul came out and talked as we prepared. "Gonna be a tough go," he drawled. "We got a lot of snow." He rolled a cigarette, then lit it. "Do you know where to go?" he asked.

"No, but we'll figure that out," we said. We were ready to go.

"Better grab some ears of corn," he said in his quiet drawl. "That bottom's awful dark." His cigarette hung on his bottom lip and it bobbed up and down as he talked.

We grabbed some corn and started out. The snow was DEEP, with some drifts up to our waists. We took our time, going short distances, then resting. I pulled the toboggan while Phil held everything steady. The going was so hard and slow, I wondered if he was RIDING on the toboggan, while my back was turned.

We finally arrived, and though we had never fished here, we knew there were pike in the lake. Before setting up our shanties we put out some tip-ups. After setting three, Phil hollered, FLAG UP! We ran to the tip-up and waited for the line to stop going out. IT stopped, then began moving again. He set the hook and lined the fish out onto the ice. We had a nice fat pike. He grinned at me with his toothless grin, then hollered at me, "NOT BAD, AYE!?"

"Ya!" I answered. "Not bad, and we've only been here ten minutes!"

"Ya!" he yelled, as he ran over to our pile of stuff. "Let's get our shanties up!"

We quickly cut our spearing holes, set our shanties up, then packed snow around the edge to block out any light. We went inside, pulled the door closed then sat down. WE COULDN'T SEE A THING! The water was so murky, we couldn't see the bottom in four foot of water. I shelled some corn and dropped it into the water. It disappeared at three foot down! I strained my eyes, in the darkness trying to see the bottom.

"Can YOU see the bottom?" I yelled at Phil.

"No, it's all murky!" he answered.

"Well, we'll have to go shallower," I said, as I dragged my shanty closer to shore, and began making another hole.

"Hey! FLAG UP!" Phil hollered. We ran over, and this time I pulled nice fat pike through the hole onto the ice.

"MAN! I'd like to spear some of these!" I said.

We finally had our shanties relocated in only two feet of water. As I again peered into my spearing hole, the water was just as black, so I dropped the corn down again. I could see where it rested on the bottom, but I thought, "Man this is shallow!"

I hooked my decoy on the treble hook and lowered him into the murk. A pike came in so FAST, I didn't have time to spear him! He smacked the decoy, sending it falling to the bottom. He came back for a second look. This time, I was ready, and shot the spear right behind his head. I flipped the pike out through my door and yelled to Phil, "I got one!"

After only two hours, we had three nice pike and totaled with six at the end of the day we'd had a hard time getting there and getting started, but it was well WORTH the EFFORT!!!

My Fish?

The lake looked beautiful, just like a picture! My wife and I had traveled for 6 hours, and we were ready to go fishing.

We were meeting my wife's sister and brother-in-law at a fishing lodge in Canada for a fishing vacation. They were to arrive later that evening, so we had the whole afternoon to fish, by ourselves.

The lake was huge, 6 miles long, and we didn't know where to fish, so we asked around. Someone told us where a tree had fallen over and was partly submerged in the lake. "That tree usually holds some walleye, and the perch are easy to catch." This was the place we were looking for. It was fairly close to camp, and we could catch fish.

We motored over to the site and began fishing. They were right we caught a few walleye and lots of perch. We'd been fishing for an hour when my wife asked me if I thought there were pike here. I told her probably, but I didn't want to fuss with another pole.

"Well," she said, "I'll rig one up. Do you have an extra pole?"

"I do."

"Do you have a treble hook and a big bobber?" she asked.

"I do," was my answer. I proceeded to hook the treble and bobber to my extra pole.

"Can you get me a small perch out of the fish basket?"

"Yeah."

"Can you hook it to the treble hook?"

"Yeah," I sighed.

"Do you think you could throw it way out from the boat so it won't be in my way?"

"Yeah." I just wanted to get on with the walleye and perch fishing.

I threw the line out, set the pole down and went back to walleye fishing.

The bobber and minnow continuously drifted toward the boat. I continuously casted it back out.

"Are you sure you want this pole out there?" I asked.

"Well just throw it out there and maybe I'll catch a big pike," she answered.

The bobber acted like the perch had gotten tangled up in a weed bed. I stood up, and reeled the line in, rapidly. When the bobber was 8 feet from the boat, I SAW something! A HUGE pike had grabbed the perch sideways in its mouth. I tried to give it some slack, but I was reeling too fast. The pike spooked when he saw the boat and me.

I threw the line back out, hoping for another strike!

About a half an hour later, my brother in law motored up and asked us if we wanted to go in and get something to eat.

"Sure," we said, then told them about the big pike. On the way over, my wife's sister had caught an 8 inch baby pike, hadn't taken it off her line, but had her pole perched over her shoulder like a Tom Sawyer pouch on a stick. It just trailed along in the water. As we sat talking, it had sunk into deep water. I had pulled anchor and began to motor backwards, so we could turn around and head for camp. We realized from a distance that their boat hadn't moved. My sister-in-law seemed to have snagged her line on a branch, below the surface. She told her husband, "I think I've snagged a log."

"Give me that pole," he said as he started pulling on the line. "There's something on the end, but it's not a snag, it's moving!"

From our boat, we watched helplessly as they fought, then landed "MY WIFE'S" fish. It was a 38 inch northern pike! It was the biggest fish caught in camp all week.

Why did my wife's face seem a bit green as we motored back for supper? Maybe it was all the trees reflecting into the water? I DOUBT IT!

Birds in the Hand

In 1966, my brothers Phil, Jim, and I woke with anticipation. It was the last Saturday of the pheasant hunting season. During the night 3 inches of snow had fallen. We weren't sure whether to go hunting, or not, but decided to try it anyway.

We arrived at our hunting spot and began walking the soggy fields, looking for birds. The wet snow had bent the grasses and weeds to the ground. We worked to the edge of the field when Kim our small dog, went on point. He usually didn't point birds but instead, would rather flush them. I ran over to him, getting ready for a shot. He held point. I looked down into the grasses and saw a mature ringneck rooster. I don't know if he couldn't or wouldn't fly. I reached down and grabbed him by the neck. I had just caught a mature ringneck rooster with my bare hands.

The next bird in my hand was a partridge in the spring. I was driving down a two track in the woods my wife and I had bought. Spring had sprung, black mushrooms were up, and the "Pats" were drumming everywhere. I noticed a male Pat running alongside my truck. I stopped my truck and he just stood there, all ruffed up. I opened my door and stuck my foot out. He attacked my foot as I slid my body out of the truck and laid on the ground. I wiggled one hand while my body remained still. He spurred my hand as I eased into a crouch, still moving my hand. He was so intent on my moving hand he never saw my other hand as I grabbed his legs. I had caught a male pat with my bare hands.

I took the bird home to show Kokie and Todd and Dave, but they were off shopping. I released the bird to go back to his courting dance. Maybe he'd be a little wiser next time.

Phantom Coon

The dogs struck the coon in the same spot as they always did, a small woods on the edge of a clear-cut. My son Todd and I were hunting our old female Bluetick Gleem, and her two pups, Hog and Dusty.

After starting the track in the small woods, they'd run it through the clear-cut. The clear-cut was 3-4 years old and very thick. They crossed the clear-cut like they were right on the coon's tail, went over a ridge, through a big woods, then back to the clear-cut. The dogs then sounded like they were miles away, then there was silence, just like they had dropped into a hole. We drove around the section listening for the dogs but we couldn't hear enough to get an accurate location.

One night Todd and I rode to the other side of the section and listened. We could faintly hear the dogs in the middle. We drove back home and dropped Todd off, for he had school in the morning.

I walked toward the dogs hoping that they'd hold the tree till I got there. As I walked toward the faint barking, I wondered what was happening with them. I could hardly hear them. I finally got to the dogs and they had a huge coon in a big broken down hollow tree. The outside had a big split in the bark just big enough for the dogs to get their noses into. They were scrambling all over each other, trying to get at the coon through the crack in the bark. Taking a stout stick, I pried the tree open and got our prize out. It was a nice big boar coon.

The other coon I ran many times but I never treed or caught that one. We'd start that coon in a small woods across from the muck fields, then cross a gravel road into the muck fields. There were times I thought the dogs would catch the coon in the field. The coon then headed back for the woods, where he came from. Then BANG! the dogs would lose him. I walked to the spot where the dogs always lost him. I tried to find his escape route but never found it.

One day while setting traps for coon in a culvert, I found the spot where the dogs had always lost the coon. The tube ran under the road. One end was high and dry and the other end was submerged under water in the muck field. The coon would run the field, head back toward the woods, slip into the pool of water, run through the culvert, then out to high ground. The dogs would run the coon, come to the submerged culvert then Bang! No more scent. They'd eventually find the track across the road but by then the coon would be so far ahead he'd make it back to his den tree safely.

A phantom coon is just a smart coon who's learned a few little tricks to escape their predators. The harder a coon, or any animal is hunted, the stronger their survival instincts become.

Fishing in Hell

My teenage son, Dave, and I had decided to float the river for pike one evening in July. I; was working in construction at the time. The hot day had turned into a much warmer evening. I had asked Dave to charge the battery for the trolling motor and get the gear around, so when I arrived home from work we would be ready to go.

We'd agreed to meet at our rendezvous point after work. He picked me up and we left my truck downriver so we'd have a ride at the end of our float.

We were excited to get started. The weather was just perfect for northern pike. They should be jumping into the boat.

We loaded our gear, then slipped the boat into the water.

After parking his truck, Dave climbed into the bow of the boat.

Meanwhile, I hooked up the electric motor, and Dave began spatting the shore with his mepps spinner. I got my pole ready, turned on the motor, and we were on our way.

The evening was beautiful. We had floated and motored about one quarter mile and each had a couple hits and caught a few small bass. It was then that I noticed that the motor sounded a little slow when it was turned on high. "You did charge the battery didn't you?"

There was a long, silent pause. "No."

I said, "Dave, if you didn't charge the battery, this is going to be a long trip downriver." It usually took 3 to 4 hours with a fresh battery, but with oars, we could make it in 4 to 5 hours.

"Dave, we DO have oars, don't we?" I asked.

"Dad, I have one oar," was his reply. We were too far to try going back upstream. All we could do was to continue downstream.

"This is going to be one long night," I thought. We had 4 hours of daylight left, and a 6 hour trip ahead.

We went as far as the battery took us, which was about halfway. We then drifted with the current for a while. We caught a couple nice pike, but then reality sank in. We weren't moving very fast and we had to get to my truck. As we began poling with one oar, darkness set in, and the whole world changed! Mosquitoes came out by the thousands! We had long pants on, but we wore only tee shirts on top. The insects were so thick that while one man poled the boat the other would smear the bugs from his working, sweaty, arms, face, back and any other exposed areas. We felt as though we were in HELL! The night was very black, the mosquitoes were thick and we were a long way from our destination! We bumped into logs, banged into the shore, and hollered at each other. We were so desperate that we tried to pull the boat when we came to a shallow spot. The mosquitoes were so thick, we would rub our arms and feel a wet, sticky mess! We were in agony!

Finally we made it to the truck. I doubt that you will ever see two men who were so glad to get onto dry ground! Our trip had started out as a beautiful journey, and turned into HELL!

This reminds me of our walk through life. We travel down our paths and rivers encountering trials along our way. We press on going through to the end. At the end is JESUS waiting with open arms in our heavenly home.

Good Night, Bad Night

Have you ever gone on a fishing trip and heard someone say, "You should have been here yesterday. The fish were really biting." The truth is, you can only go fishing, or hunting, when you have the opportunity, or time. You have to take the good with the bad days.

I had been coon hunting for a month, and the coon were prime. The dogs were really doing well, for I hadn't had a deer or a possum chase in a couple of weeks. Coon hunting was a lot of fun. I'd eat supper, load the dogs, and off I'd go. The dogs would strike a track, while I sat back and listened to the race until they treed.

We were sitting at the supper table when I asked Kokie, my wife to go hunting with me that night. I had explained how well everything had been going. The next couple of nights were going to be beautiful weather, so she agreed to go with me.

We heard the dogs strike a track, in the woods behind the house, as we walked out of the garage. They ran for a short while then they treed. I looked at her and smiled. "See how easy this is?" I asked.

She said "I GUESS SO!"

On the way to the dogs, we came to a thick patch of Russian Olive. This is a nasty shrub which the DNR planted for deer and turkey cover. The plantings have grown so well that they've pretty much taken over many of southern Michigan's open areas. They grow to 15 feet in height, and have red fall berries, that wildlife love. They also have thorny branches, which makes them an impenetrable thicket. The tree that the critter had chosen was in the middle of one of these thickets. We had to get to the dogs, but the only way was to crawl 75 yards through the Russian Olive brush.

When we finally made it to the tree, I was eager to show her the coon. We shined the tree and there he was, A BIG OLD POSSUM! I was so disappointed, and she was SO scratched up! We leashed the dogs, then crawled back to the woods.

As I released the dogs again, I turned to her and said, "Wouldn't you know. I've gone two weeks without a trashy night, then I take someone along, and the dogs mess up!" We hunted for another two hours. The whole night was a wreck. The dogs wanted to run possum and possum they ran! We crawled on our hands and knees through thicket after thicket. My wife finally said she'd had enough. "I can't understand how you can like this," she said.

When I turned to look at her, I understood why. Her hair was a mess, thorns, twigs and leaves were everywhere. "Well, it's not always like this," I said. "I haven't had a night like this in two weeks."

The best part was that I was able to hunt the good AND the bad nights. I was able to say to someone, "You should have been with me LAST night. IT WAS BEAUTIFUL!"

Jim

The decoy pulled on the line, as the pike slowly slid into the shanty hole from the front. "SEE HIM?" I asked Jim.

"Yeah."

I slowly took the spear, dipping the tines in the water, then threw it. I missed! We looked at each other and shook our heads.

We were spearing Podunk Lake by Hastings. Big pike. Big, big bass in very murky water. We had to drop corn, potatoes, and newspapers, to the bottom, just to see. We speared many fish here. We'd spear all day, then around four o'clock we'd go to our bluegill holes to fish for bluegill.

We were looking for new lakes to spear, when we heard that Gun Lake was open to spearing. Gun had been closed to spearing for 15 years. The DNR had planted musky in Gun for many years. The locals were complaining that there weren't any panfish left so the DNR opened it to the spearers.

We set our shanties on the south-east end off the State Park peninsula. The bright green cabbage weeds were brilliant in the crystal clear water. We sat in the deep water, here, for a couple of days, but I didn't spear any fish, so I decided to move to Baird's cove. I set up in the middle of 40-50 shanties. I was in 5 feet of water, with a nice sandy bottom. Jim meanwhile decided to stay in the deep water.

The morning was sunny, as all of us spearers readied our shanties for the day. A half hour later everyone had settled down, the stoves were lit, coffee poured. We were staring at the bottom, when craaaaack craaaaaack, a couple of big pressure cracks ran diagonally through all the shanties.

Everyone rushed out of their shanties wondering why the 8 inches of clear hard ice had cracked.

Then we saw it! A yellow Duster was driving toward us on the ice, pulling a shanty. Jim had decided to move and hadn't felt like dragging his shanty by hand so he hooked it to his car! He kept right on coming in spite of all the cursing and fists raised. There were 40 irate spearers and one happy one.

Too Late!

I was getting frantic as I looked for my treestand. "Why? Why do people have to steal tree-stands on state land?" I thought. I knew that I should have locked it up.

I had risen early to give myself plenty of time to have a cup of coffee, then headed for my stand. I was walking one mile to my stand before daylight on the opening morning of bowhunting. Now, here I was, sweating and frantically shining pine trees, looking for my stand. My coveralls were wide open and sweat was running freely. A rooster crowed at a neighboring farm. "TIME! It's time to climb, NOW!" I thought. I frantically searched along the deer trail which my stand was supposed to have overlooked.

Two days earlier, I had placed markers of broken pine twigs on different trees at ten, twenty, and thirty yard intervals. I spotted my thirty yard marker, then the twenty, then the ten. Ahead my light shone to "my tree." There it was, and my stand was still there! Sweating profusely by now, I hurriedly walked to my tree and prepared to climb. After climbing up, I pulled up my bow then sat back trying to relax. By now, I had all my shirts, and coverall, wide open. My glasses were fogged up and my hair was dripping wet.

I had climbed too late! I just knew I had. Oh, well. I'd sit back and watch the morning unfold. I could now make out the forms of trees through the darkness.

"Oh, well, maybe next time," I thought. WAIT! Was that a deer, sneaking down the trail? I grabbed my bow from its hook, knocked an arrow, and drew back. The deer was at my twenty yard marker. As he cleared a tree, I released my arrow. THUD! The deer took off on a run. I had hit something but couldn't see well enough to tell where, or what. I'd have to wait until light to look for blood.

The rising sun lit the woods as I prepared to climb down to check for blood. Then I saw it. My arrow, fifteen feet in front of me, was stuck in a pine tree. There was no need to climb down, now.

"Oh, well. I blew that one. I had my chance and lost it. I might as well hang it up," I thought. The dawn temperature was cooling me down now, so I buttoned my shirts back up and zipped my coverall and waited a bit longer.

As a red squirrel moved from pine to pine, chattering his disapproval, and a "pat" drummed in the distance, I thought back to something my wife had asked me when we were first married. "Honey," she said, "who has an old John Deere tractor around here? I don't know why, but every morning, at the same time, they start it up, then after a short time, they just turn it off."

"Yeah. That's a pat alright," I thought.

I was settled down now. The sweat had dried and I was even a little chilly.

Suddenly, A DEER! Another deer was coming down the trail! "Calm down. It's a decent buck," I told myself. I drew, held steady, and waited for a clear shot. Anchor, steady, release. My mind marched through the steps. This time the deer fell on the spot. I had hit his spine. He fell like a rock, then began thrashing around on the ground. Nocking another arrow I shot again. It flew over the deer as he thrashed his way down the hill. I shot once more and missed again. Having shot all my arrows, I lowered my bow, watching him thrash farther down the hill.

I reached into my pocket for my knife, which was a small pocket knife, not big enough to finish off a buck who had full control of his head. "Useless," I thought.

I ran over to the deer and he lunged at me with his antlers. I grabbed a stout stick, thinking that I could wedge it in his rack and turn his head, cutting off his air. I twisted his head around and waited, and waited. "This isn't going to work," I thought.

I was out of arrows and I couldn't find any that I'd shot at him earlier. But WAIT! I still had one stuck in a tree from my first shot! I climbed that tree, grabbed the arrow, ran back to the deer and finished him off.

Kneeling down, I admired my buck in the morning light. It was a nice, high racked six point, and was I ever glad that I hadn't gotten to my stand "TOO LATE."

Spring Birds

The spring of 2000 was the year of the birds. Hoping to attract bluebirds, I had built ten bluebird houses the previous winter and placed them all over our farm. After a rather warm winter, spring finally came, and we had fun watching the various species compete for all the new housing. Starlings were the first to arrive. People generally don't like starlings, but we have come to appreciate them. God created everything, and called it good, but we always wondered what was good about starlings!

Having moved to the Central Michigan area, we were in the process of remodeling an old, foursquare, stone farmhouse. While working on it, the doors were often open as we went in and out. We began to notice a lot of flies, and after some inquiries, discovered that they were called cluster flies. These flies, by the hundreds, would be clustered in the corners of rooms, and on all the windows. They were everywhere! We sealed up all of the cracks/windows, etc. We tuckpointed all of the stones on the outside of the house. We finally resorted for fly parasites from a garden catalogue. We loosed them into the attic and they did the job inside the walls of the house. The flies continued to live, over the winter, in all of the old barns and outbuildings, though. They would come out in the early, sunny days of spring, and the grasses were full of them! While the mornings were still cold, we noticed that the starlings would walk in flocks through the yard and feed on them. Thank you, Starlings! Phoebes were also attracted to the flies, so we built nesting sites for them under the eaves of the porch. Blue birds also feasted on them.

Up and down, up and down, from the fence to the ground, all day long they feasted this helped a lot. God's word says that He leads the birds to where they can find food, and we have prayed for God to get rid of the flies for us, because we couldn't. We know He sent these birds to us.

We came to appreciate the starling flocks especially, as there had begun an infestation of June bug grubs in our side yard. The starlings, with their long white beaks, would poke along into the ground and eliminate the beetles as they began to surface in mid-spring. Again, thank you starlings! They were ingenious birds, and found every available crook and cranny to nest in, but we didn't mind them nesting under the eaves of the outbuildings. A pair found one permanent yearly niche in a knothole, in the grainery siding. We welcome their presence each spring. They'd tried to claim some of the houses I'd made but couldn't fit through the openings.

We were excited when the bluebirds finally arrived. The males went from house to house, all excited about their find. Other birds, such as chirping sparrows and house finches, weren't excited about their arrival. The starlings weren't happy about their presence either, and we watched a few battles for territory. The bluebirds didn't like all the competition and moved on. We now had ten vacant houses. House finches claimed one. They also built a nest under the front porch eaves, and one in the large spruce next to the house. These rosy-breasted little birds are delightful creatures with a very nice song. The females are brownish in color.

The next birds we watched, while raising their young, were a pair of Kestrels. The year before, we'd had a barn full of pigeons, which messed over everything, so I closed up the siding on the barn. My wife liked having some pigeons around, so I thought about a way to create a nesting site for them. I climbed way up to the peak of the barn's gable end. I made a nesting box on an inside platform, then made a hole in the siding for the birds to get into. I then placed a board, from the inside of the nest to the outside, for a perch. The pigeons tried the nestbox. They went in a few times but never nested. Later, we noticed a small hawk on the perch. We continued to watch daily as a pair of Kestrels carried nesting materials into the box. They loved the site. As spring progressed we watched the pair as the male carried food for the female on the nest.

When the chicks finally hatched, we watched as both parents diligently brought food to their young. The first chick came outside on June 1. He stood on that high perch, just looking around, waiting for his parents to arrive with food. He waited on that perch until he saw mom or dad, then he would run back into the hole and begin to screech. The parents would fly at the opening, fold their wings, tae one hop on the perch, and they were in, all in one fluid motion. All the chicks finally made it out onto the perch, and they'd all sit there like three gray furry balls lined up in a row, watching the world. They finally left us. One day they were all on the perch in their feathered plumage, and the next day they were gone.

The tree swallows were the most interesting birds of all to me. They used four of the houses for nesting. They are the acrobats of the bird world. They can climb straight up, swoop down, and turn on a dame! They have to be able to catch mosquitoes and small bugs on the fly, and this is quite a job when there are four or five chicks to feed!

Next to my garden, there is a birdhouse which we can see from out back deck. We spent many an hour watching their acrobatics. While the Kestrels were still nesting, we saw many air duels. Both birds could really maneuver in the air, but the hawks never came close to catching a swallow!

That year, I spent a lot of time in my garden planting corn, weeding, and tending tomatoes. There were times, when I was working within a few feet of the birdhouses, that I could hear the peeping of the chicks as the parents returned to feed them. One day as I was hoeing corn, the male swooped down CLOSE, almost hitting my face. He flew straight at me, turning upwards at the last second, while letting out a loud chatter! He did this over and over until I ran out of the garden! I thought this was a one time deal, but every time I went back he did the same thing! I thought the young must be getting ready to fly and he didn't want any intruders. As soon as the young were airborne, we got along just fine.

A pair of Pheobe flycatchers nested in the basement of the barn, on top of a large beam. I'd leave the barn doors open just a crack, so they could fly in and out. One day, as I went in to get a tool, I noticed that the fledglings were flying around. They were banging into the window panes trying to get out. I opened both of the big barn doors, hoping they would fly out, but they kept hitting the windows. I caught two of them with my hands and let them out the door. The third one found the door and left on its own.

The final group of birds that I remember returning and nesting that spring were the Killdeers. They came back screaming "KILLDEER!" "KILLDEER!" They thought every patch of gravel was a nesting spot, driveways, two tracks, gardens, They would run around acting injured whenever we came close to their "chosen" spot! Opening one wing until it dragged the ground, they'd cry out and toddle away like a drunken sailor!

I knew one pair was nesting in the garden, but couldn't find the nest. I had to rototill the corn, so I asked my wife if she'd look for the nest. After hunting for an hour, and not finding it, she gave up. I said, "Oh well, if I hit it, I hit it. At least we tried." I rototilled the garden never finding the nest. A few days later I was hoeing the corn, and there it was! Between two stalks of corn lay four speckled eggs, safe and sound.

All in all, we had fun with our new birdhouses and their occupants that summer. Here's a list of the birds we housed that year.

1 CHIPPING SPARROW
1 WREN
5 TREE SWALLOWS
1 HOUSE FINCH

One Shot

"When I have a legal doe permit, I can't hit the deer!" Ed said. We were finishing Thanksgiving dinner when the talk strayed to deer hunting.

"How many deer did you miss?" I asked.

"I can't even count!" Ed said with his usual good-natured chuckle. I had set him in my deer blind earlier in the day. It was on a wooded ridge overlooking a field and a hollow, where the deer crossed. I then walked through the surrounding woods, jumping deer, and hoping he could've gotten a shot.

"I'm going to sight my gun in when I get home," Ed said. He and his wife had to leave after dinner.

My 15-year-old son, Todd, asked Ed if he'd seen any squirrels.

"Yeah," he replied, "but I wasn't squirrel hunting!" He laughed again.

We waved goodbye as Ed and Joy pulled out of the drive. "Dad," Todd turned to me and said, "I think I'll go back to your blind to get some of those squirrels." I told him he could take a single shot 12 gauge and some buckshot if he wanted to, in case he saw some deer. He headed for the blind with 4 buckshot in his left pocket and 4 birdshot in his right. He got comfortable in the chair, but didn't load the gun. He set 4 buckshot on one shelf and 4 birdshot on the other.

The afternoon sun was low when Todd noticed a group of guys on a ridge 300 yards away. They had walkie-talkies, and were moving slowly through the woods, which was hilly with ridges and valleys.

"Dummies!" he thought. "They're going to scare all the deer and squirrel away!"

Just then, he caught movement in the field to his left. Deer! The lead doe was moving carefully and quietly along the edge, and a whole herd of deer followed her. As Todd watched the herd, he saw no antlers right away. His eyes strained. A buck! The last one was a buck. A nice buck! He loaded the single with buckshot, aimed and fired. The buck hunched up, but ran off. Todd grabbed another shell, and fired at the fleeing buck. A clean miss!

His thoughts raced as he inspected the ground where the buck had been. "I hit him!" He tracked blood into a button bush swamp, where the deer had stumbled down. He saw it, alive, but clearly, badly hurt. He reached for shells. His pockets were empty! He's left them back at the blind! Running towards the buck, his eyes searched for a club. There was nothing heavy enough. "I've got a stout club right here!" he thought, as his arms raised instinctively above his head.

No knife! Now he'd have to drag the buck home before he could gut it out.

My wife was looking out the sliding glass doors when she saw him. "Honey, come here," she said. "Todd is stumbling around, and it looks like he's hurt!"

I rushed to look, and shouted, "He's got a deer!"

Todd was dragging the whole deer, 15 feet at a time, stumbling and falling as he went, from the exhaustion.

We ran down to him, and then saw his deer was a nice 8 point buck! He then told us his story of how he'd chased it, fallen down a hill, and broke my gun in the process.

Eight years later, as we were opening gifts at Christmas, Todd presented me with a new, single, 12 gauge shotgun.

"What's this?" I asked.

"Well," he said slowly, "you know the gun I shot that 8 point buck with?"

"Yeah," I replied.

"Well, I didn't fall down and break it. I clubbed the deer with it, so here is your replacement!"

Rol Nibbs

As I was driving along the back roads of Clay Hills, near Middleville, I saw an old man hobbling along the edge of the road. He was using a walking stick for a cane. He flagged me down and asked me if I'd drive him to town for a few supplies. As he eased into my car, I noticed his dropsy-swollen lower legs and ankles. He did his shopping and we returned to his house. The ramshackle home of this old bachelor was gray and bare-looking in the woods that surrounded it.

We learned from an older neighbor lady that when he was young he fell in love with a girl named Gertie, who married someone else. He never married.

He sold his land to the State and had a life lease on the house, living a very lonely, cold existence.

Sometimes I checked on him, when I was hunting in his area. I often lit the fire in his old wood stove. I liked that stove and asked if he'd like to sell it. "Oh, no!" he said. "I can't sell that!"

My wife and I had been engaged for a couple of months, and Thanksgiving was just around the corner. We decided that Rol could use a nice Thanksgiving dinner. Kokie prepared it all, including the pie and stuffing. That evening, we started out from Grandville, and it began to storm. It snowed heavily and we had some trouble driving on those wooded back roads. The heavy flakes, and driving wind nearly whited out everything in our head-lights. Arriving at his house, we found it all closed up and dark, with no smoke coming from the chimney. We were disappointed he wasn't home and ended up sitting in his snow filled driveway, eating the dinner in the car by headlights.

When Rol's health got worse and he was placed in a nursing home, he gave me the stove and his shotgun to keep until he could return 'home.'

After our twins were born, he stopped by during one of his visits to his old hoe. He wanted to see our twins, and was very happy when we said, "Sure! Come right on in."

He shuffled down the hall, leaned over both bassinettes, and with delight, he said, "Dandy babies! Dandy babies!" He was rough-shorn and toothless, but had a tender, good heart.

Rol passed away at the nursing home and I have his stove and gun yet today.

CPSIA information can be obtained at www.ICGtesting.com
Printed in the USA
BVOW082126090812

297529BV00007B/46/P